Our New Baby

Words by Jan Grant

Pictures by Phillip Lanier

CHILDRENS PRESS, CHICAGO

3 4 5 6 7 8 9 10 11 12 R 86 85 84

Library of Congress Cataloging in Publication Data

Grant, Jan.
Our new baby.

SUMMARY: A young child doesn't understand why her parents want a new baby when they already have her.
[1. Babies—Fiction] I. Lanier, Phillip.
II. Title.
PZ7.G766758Ou [E] 79-22048
ISBN 0-516-01480-3

Our New Baby

My mom is going to have a baby. The baby is growing inside of her. That's why she looks the way she does.

Mom and Dad are always busy now. Today I wanted Dad to play with me. But he said, "Not now. I am painting this old dresser for the new baby." Mom can't play either. She is sorting baby clothes. Everyone is busy doing something for the new baby. No one has time for me.

SORRY!
SORRY!
CHUTES LADDERS
Perfection
Perfection
memory
GOLDILOCKS THREE BEARS
GOLDILOCKS THREE BEARS
BINGO

Last week Mom and Dad brought my old cradle down from the attic. They put it in my room. Dad said, "You'll have to share your room with the new baby until we can afford a bigger house."

I had to move all my things to one side of the room. I don't want to share my room with a baby.

Mom and Dad think it's going to be fun having a new baby around. They spend hours and hours just talking about names for the baby. I don't think it will be very much fun at all!

"Why do you want a new baby when you already have me?" I asked Mom.

"You're not a baby anymore," she answered. "You're a big girl. You can do lots of things a baby can't do. I am very proud of you and all the things you can do. I would be very lonely without you to keep me company."

One day I went with Mom to the doctor's office. I had to wait outside while she went in to see Dr. Foley.

After a while, Dr. Foley came out and asked me to come inside. He asked me how I felt about getting a new brother or sister.

"Sometimes having a new baby in the family takes some getting used to," said Dr. Foley. "It's not always easy. A new baby can be a lot of work. Babies need lots of time and care and love. The new baby in your family will be lucky to have a big sister like you."

Then Dr. Foley gave me a book about babies to take home.

Dr. Foley let me listen to the baby's heartbeat through a stethoscope.

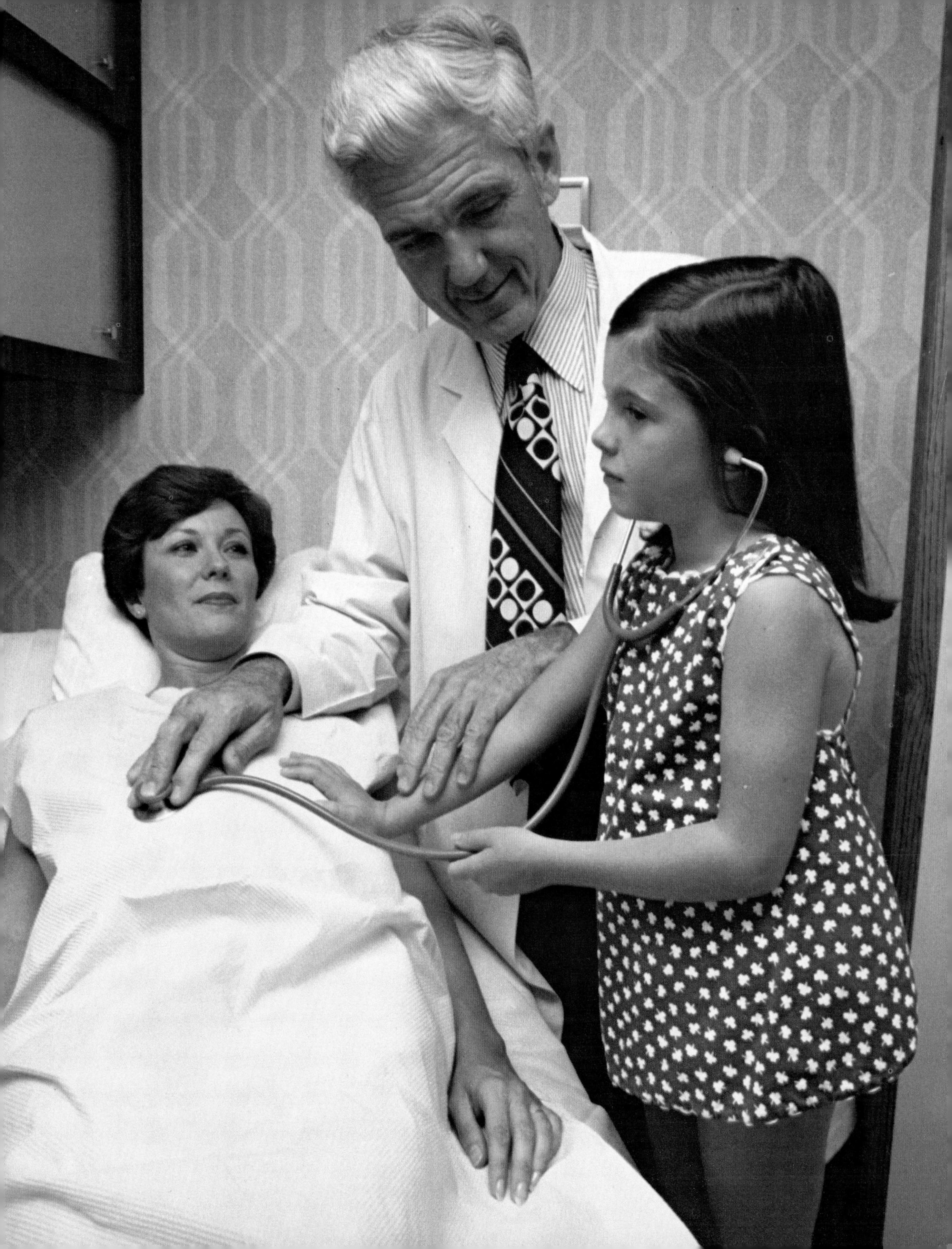

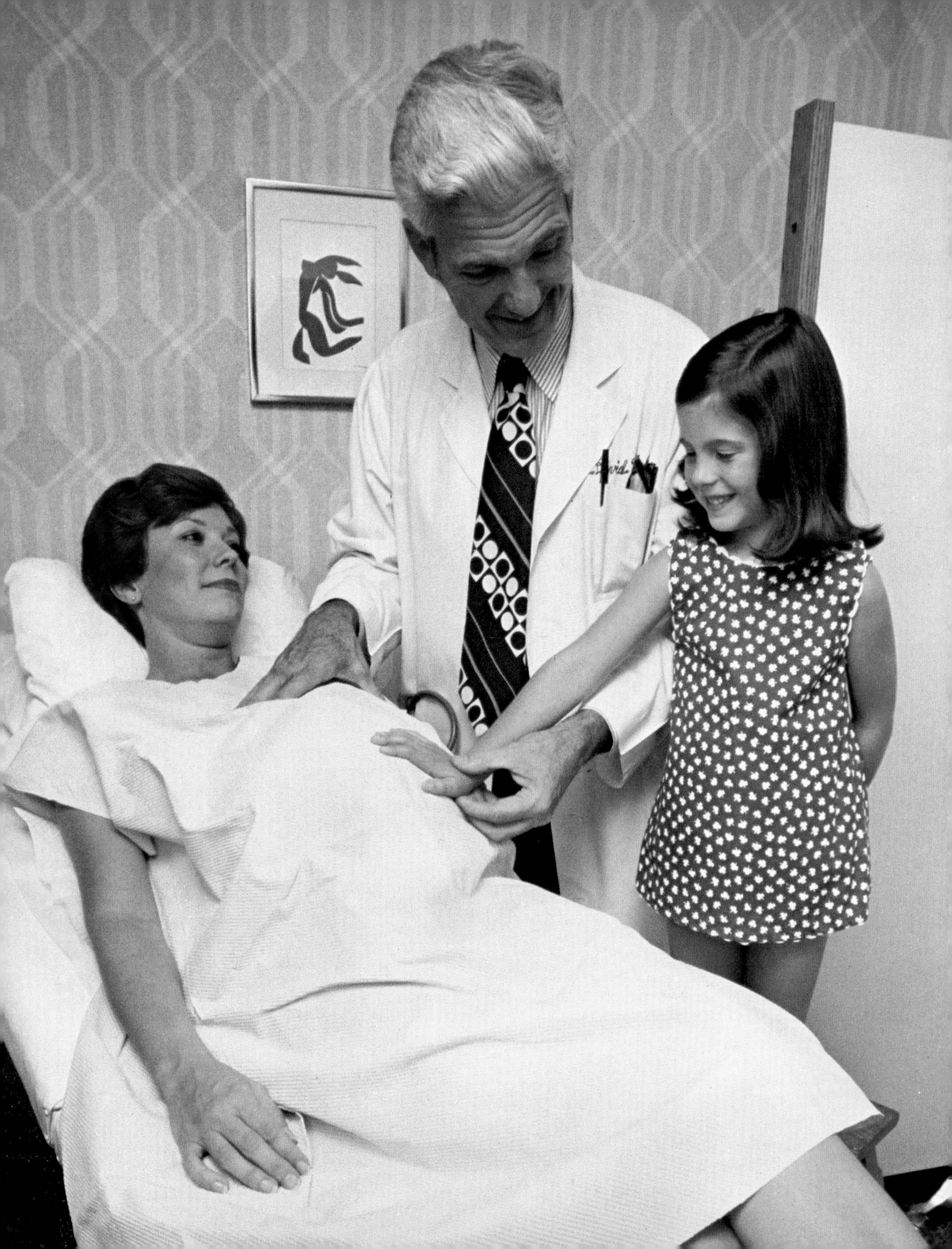

I put my hand on Mom's stomach. I could feel the baby move.

I felt a lot better when I left Dr. Foley's office.

On Sunday, Mom had to go to the hospital in a hurry. She knew the baby wanted to be born. Dad went with her. Grandma came to stay with me.

The next day the people at the hospital let me look at my new brother through a window. Then a nurse took me to visit Mom in a special room.

"I want you to come home now," I told her.

"I will come home with your new brother in a few days," said Mom. "Your new brother's name is Steven. What do you think of him?"

"He doesn't look like much. I thought he would be bigger," I told her. "He's too small to play with me."

Many people came to our house to see Steven. They all brought presents for him. No one brought a present for me. Everyone wanted to hold Steven. The grown-ups kept making silly noises at him and calling him names like "Pumpkin." Why was everyone making such a fuss? He's just a dumb old baby. He can't even do anything. Boy did I get angry.

After the people left, Mom asked me to sit in the chair with her. She told me what it was like when I was a baby.

I didn't know that people brought lots of presents for me. "Some of the things that Steven will use were given to you when you were a baby," said Mom.

Mom told me that when I was a baby, Grandma and Grandpa always wanted to hold me. Mom said she hardly got a chance to hold me herself.

Mom and I laughed about the funny things I did when I was a baby. I asked Mom to tell me the story over and over again.

Then Steven began to cry. Mom gave him some milk to drink. Dad changed his diaper. But he kept on crying. He would not stop. Mom put Steven in his cradle. Still he cried and cried. Then I had an idea. I rocked the cradle and started to sing my favorite song. Soon Steven stopped crying. Boy, were Mom and Dad surprised! I think Mom and Dad are really going to need my help with our new baby.